M

is for Autism

of related interest

Haze
Kathy Hoopmann
ISBN 978 1 84310 072 0
eISBN 978 1 84642 405 2

Blue Bottle Mystery
Kathy Hoopmann
ISBN 978 1 85302 978 3
eISBN 978 1 84642 169 3

The Adventure of Maisie Voyager
Lucy Skye
ISBN 978 1 84905 287 0
eISBN 978 0 85700 604 2

Freaks, Geeks and Asperger Syndrome
A User Guide to Adolescence
Luke Jackson
ISBN 978 1 84310 098 0
eISBN 978 1 84642 356 7

M

is for Autism

The Students of
Limpsfield Grange School
and Vicky Martin

Illustrated by the Students of
Limpsfield Grange School
and Luna Pérez Visairas

Foreword by Robert Pritchett

Jessica Kingsley *Publishers*
London and Philadelphia

First published in 2015
by Jessica Kingsley Publishers
73 Collier Street
London N1 9BE, UK
and
400 Market Street, Suite 400
Philadelphia, PA 19106, USA

www.jkp.com

Library of Congress Cataloging in Publication Data
A CIP catalog record for this book is available
from the Library of Congress

British Library Cataloguing in Publication Data
A CIP catalogue record for this book is
available from the British Library

ISBN 978 1 84905 684 7
eISBN 978 1 78450 198 3

Printed and bound in Great Britain

The students and staff of Limpsfield Grange School would like to thank Autism Accreditation for supporting our project. Without them M's story would never have been fully realised. We are really grateful to have been given this opportunity to tell her amazing story.

Foreword

At a National Autistic Society Autism Accreditation sharing practice meeting in the summer of 2014, Beth and Máire, two remarkable and articulate teenage girls from Limpsfield Grange School, spoke to us about how their autism affects them. It was extraordinary, illuminating and moving. Afterwards, Beth told me that there were no books to help teenage girls with autism. Someone, she said, should write one. Máire, who is a remarkable artist, added that it should be illustrated. The answer was obvious, and we decided there and then that Autism Accreditation should sponsor the Limpsfield Grange girls to do just that. Write a book written and illustrated entirely *by* teenage girls with autism *for* teenage girls with autism.

The early teen years can be tough for girls with autism as they learn to understand themselves, the changes they are going through and the changing expectations the world has of them. Autism adds another complication. The girls passionately want people to understand them and to help other girls with autism understand themselves. That would make a big difference to their lives. M's story is the wonderful result! The Limpsfield girls certainly found their voice and it has all the urgency, immediacy and sheer vibrancy of teenage life.

The process of writing the book was a collaboration between the students of Limpsfield Grange and writer Vicky Martin, who led creative writing and drama workshops to explore situations the students had experienced and to express how it really feels to be an autistic teenage girl. Through improvisations, story writing, poetry and discussion, M began to take shape and tell her important story.

I must thank Beth, whose idea it was to write a book in the first place; Sarah Wild, the Head Teacher, who agreed to the project; and of course all the staff and students at Limpsfield Grange.

I hope that M's journey will help girls with autism making that same journey through their early teen years to find themselves and believe in themselves as well as to help others understand and believe in them. As Beth said, "The trouble is some people do get me but many more don't."

Robert Pritchett, Director, Autism Accreditation

M's Introduction

I've been pushed into a
room and I'm stuck.

I can see through the windows
but I can't open them and I
don't even know if I can see
the same objects, people
and colours as you...

I'm just not sure. I'm locked in
and I don't have a key to get out.

M. That's what I'd like you to call me please. M. I'll tell you why later. In fact, I'll be telling you lots about me and my **tipsy-turvy, wobbly world**. My beautiful, terrifying, stressful, difficult, anxious life. I mean, I am just like any other teenage girl. I want to fit in, have friends and wear nice clothes. I want to be liked and I have ambitions, plans and hopes. I go to school and live with my mad family but the difference is I deal with so many more shapes, sizes, noises, colours, textures and anxieties than you may ever know.

You might know a girl like me or maybe you are just like me too...

Chapter 1

I'm in a forest. It's very noisy. Disturbing.

There are lots of other animals in the forest but I feel like I'm a different species to all the others.

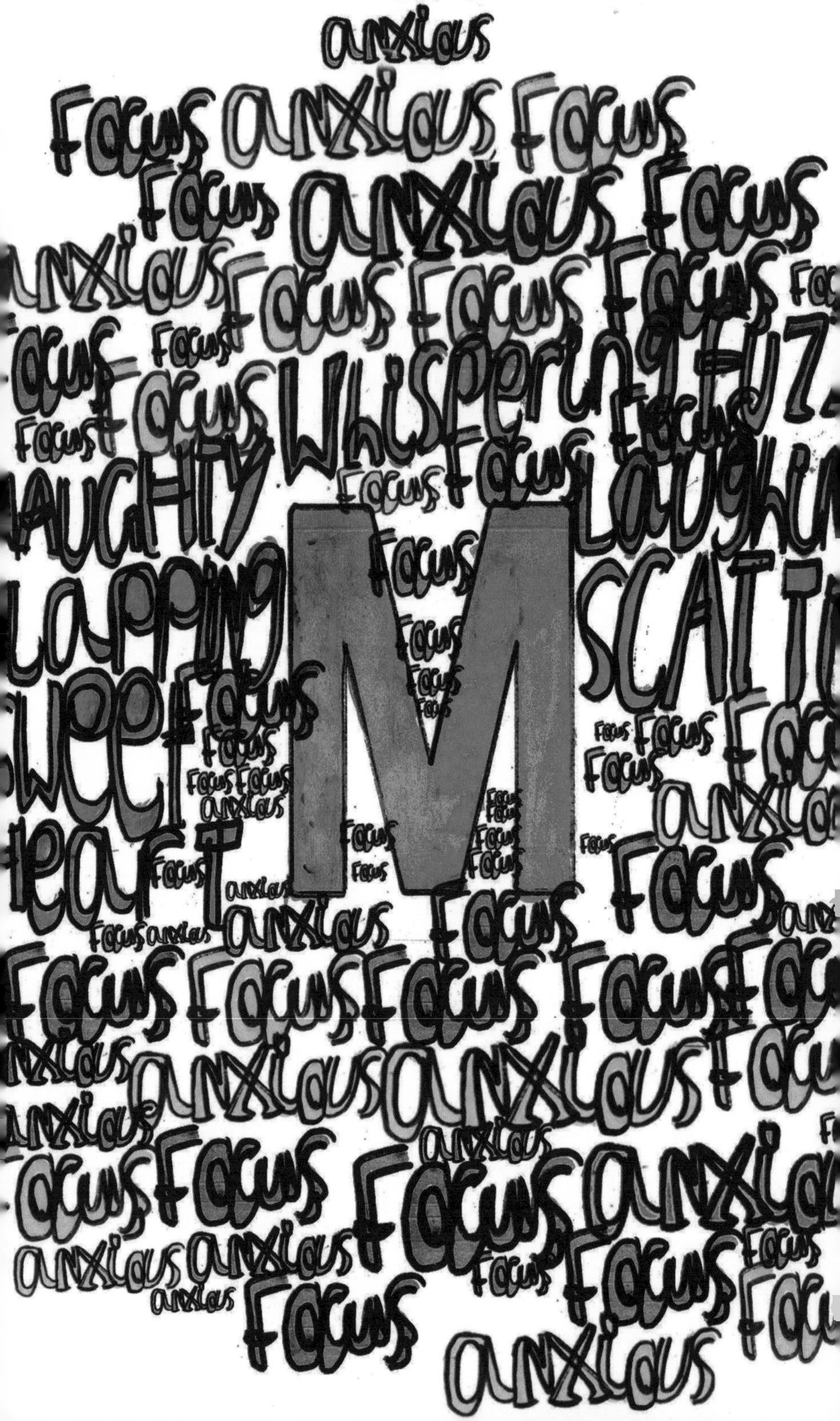
anxious
focus
Whispering
M

This is when I became **M**. I wasn't named M. I chose it and this is how it happened. One Monday afternoon. I was in Year 5 and we were working on number sequencing in the morning and it was spelling tests in the afternoon. I hadn't slept all weekend because my anxiety was so high. In fact, I know I've just started my story but I think we should stop here – for the time being.

You see I use the word anxiety and this is the biggest word, thing, emotion, part of my life. Maybe you are one of the people who says,

"Oh dear, poor thing, you'll be fine. It's just a bit of stress." Or maybe you're the type of person who looks at me seething and thinks I should pull myself together and stop making a fuss because I am ruining everything for everyone else. Selfish!

I'm used to hearing and sensing both these responses and neither of them make the situation any better because my anxiety is so massive, so consuming and controlling. I looked up anxiety in the dictionary and this is what it says:

Anxiety [noun]

1. A feeling of worry, nervousness, or unease about something with an uncertain outcome: "She felt a surge of anxiety."

But this is what I say:

<u>Anxiety [noun]</u>

1. An uncontrollable, wild, savage beast that prowls beside me taking me hostage at it's will. Can make frenzied attacks which strangle the life out of me. Stops me walking, talking or seeing or hearing. It shakes my brain, my inner core and rattles my nerves. Inflicts terror, causes chaos and prevents a normal existence.

So, I hope you can see it's not possible for me to just pull myself together, as I haven't worked out how to control this force, this frenzied, cruel beast. Sorry to interrupt you with anxiety but it interrupts me all day long... So, back to the spelling test. The words had been jangling round my head all weekend.

Angry, alarm, angel, absent, ANXIOUS, able, anaconda, area.

I couldn't sit still. Fidgeting. I was **PaNiCKing**.

Miss Haynes said, "Focus! **FOCUS!**"

At lunch a teacher said I was naughty. **NAUGHTY** because I couldn't eat.

"Has the cat got your tongue?" asked the bus driver this morning.

I was crying because no one sat next to me on the "Friendship Bench" in the playground. Someone is always meant to sit next to you when you sit on the "Friendship Bench."

The TA called me sca-t-tY.

One girl was whispering about me to the other girls.

"Stop flapping your hands sweetheart," said the dinner lady.

I sat at my table trying to focus on my spellings. Miss Haynes said,

"Antennae. Spell antennae."

I could sense anxiety circling around the classroom. Its eyes locked on me, getting nearer and nearer and the bright sunlight kept hitting me in my eyes making everything look fuzzy.

Antennae.

I knew this. I had practised this all weekend but I was on overload now. All these words and letters crammed in my head but I couldn't get them out. They were all trapped, locked in my skull! I squeezed my silver pen in between my fingers and thumb but I couldn't move it. I couldn't get the letters out! And the boy beside me kept repeating the word over and over again to me. He said he was trying to HELP ME.

I just want to be like everyone else and do the test! I just want to be normal.

Fidgeting. Panicking. Focus. FOCUS! Naughty. SCAtty. Whispering, Laughing. The cat? Sweetheart. Fuzzy. Flapping. Help me. Antennae. Again and again.

Why can't I be normal? I looked up...

All the letters in the alphabet were stuck around the classroom wall, you know,

A for Apple, D for Dancing, and then I noticed **M** in the middle of the alphabet.

M with all the other letters either side of it, crushing, jostling and pressing against it.

M trapped. How could the letter M ever hope to escape with those other letters shoving, shouldering and squeezing it into the middle? Pushing against it and keeping M in the middle. Stuck in the middle. And that's how I felt. Getting crushed and hurt and stuck and trapped.

M stuck in the Middle M. In a Muddle. Me in the middle.

I wanted to bolt! Run away from that room in my pretty, patent shoes. But I knew I would be told off again and anyway anxiety was trapping me as it slid its strong arm around my little neck and squeezed. I could hardly breathe. The classroom was quiet as everyone wrote down words in their little spelling books. I dropped my pen, it chimed as it landed on the wooden floor and loudly it rolled across the room towards Miss Haynes. She picked the pen up and shouted,

"You're being so naughty!"

Anxiety squeezed harder. So I stopped and I removed myself from this situation, from the terror. I just couldn't function. I had been rendered defunct. Not fit for purpose. I so wanted to do the spelling test but it was impossible. I didn't move my chair or anything. I don't need to...

I went off to my own little world, **MOLW**. (More about that later.) But for now, let me tell you, it's a place I fit in. It's a safe place.

And after that day, I stopped answering to the name my mum and dad gave me. Some people asked questions but I never explained and after a while everyone called me M. Even teachers when they call out the register.

After the day of the spelling test Mrs Clarke, the headmistress at my primary school, suggested I,

"Talk to someone."

But I don't talk very much, so I wasn't sure this was going to be a good idea and I wasn't sure why I had to talk someone. Like I was the problem.

Tuesday 4.00pm

So I go and see a counsellor every Tuesday after school, at 4.00. My grandma pays for me to go. She said she wanted to help. She wants me to be a happy, carefree girl... So do I. So I agreed to go.

The counsellor's room has powder blue coloured walls and a white ceiling and she is always calm. She is called Fiona. I didn't talk for the first few weeks. It was all very overwhelming. The counsellor sat opposite me on a comfy, beige, chair and said it was OK if I didn't want to talk but she was providing a safe place for me to express my feelings and to sort things out that confuse me, when I am ready. A safe place. I liked that, so after a few weeks I realised that she was always in the same seat and was always waiting for me at 4.00 on Tuesdays and I liked this, so I spoke. I asked,

"Why am I the problem? Isn't the dinner lady, the whispering girls and Miss Haynes – aren't they the problem?"

There was a silence in the powder blue room.

(I now call it the **COUNSELLOR SILENCE**; she does this sometimes when she wants me to think about things.)

"How lovely to hear your voice M," she said. "And yes, you are right, well worked out, you are not a problem."

And after a few more weeks I realised that she believed everything I said. She believed me when I told her about my anxiety and not understanding people. So I talked about more things and when she asked about my name I told her about the spelling test day and how I chose my name, and she said I'm trying to take control of my life and my identity. She's probably right. She also said it's very honest of me to call myself a name that really represents me and my feelings.

But to be honest, she doesn't know the half of it.

Chapter 2

Why do I feel so different
to everyone else?

I'm just trying to be normal.
How do I get normal?

I have an older brother. He's called **Toby** and he's what you might call normal but that doesn't make him a nice person. Most of the time he winds me up. He stays with Dad most weekends (thank God) and he says I'm the reason Dad left because I caused so much stress in the family. Toby wins lots of certificates and Mum sticks them on the fridge door with her funny little magnets of lighthouses and Buddhist phrases like, "Practise compassion and you practise love."

Toby wins certificates for maths, football, writing, most polite boy (I don't know how he won that), drama, most punctual, most helpful (really?). I told him he should win a certificate for most irritating, obnoxious, noisy brother and he pointed out that I don't get certificates, just letters home about my "challenging" behaviour or the need for "extra support" in the classroom. It's true and these letters don't make it to the fridge door, Mum shoves those in her handbag or a drawer. So when Toby came home with another certificate for being Year 10's "Top Scientist," Mum was so happy. She kept saying how proud she was,

"Toby, you're so clever. You could be a lawyer or an engineer, such a brainy boy Toby. You get all your talents from uncle Pete." Then Mum does what she always does, she looks at me, her face drops and she says she feels so guilty! And she hugs me and goes all gushy as she puts her arms all over my pink mohair jumper and her hands crush my gold, heart chain into my neck.

"I'm so sorry! You're talented too M. You're so kind M. I know you have your..." And she hesitates to find a word. "...challenges, but you're the kindest, most sensitive girl I know and that's the best talent anyone could have."

But I wasn't feeling very kind, as I stood there being hugged by Mum. I've told her so many times I don't like to be hugged or touched but she doesn't listen and still she continued to SQUEEZE me. I was feeling jealous and angry. In fact enraged, and frustrated, not kind! I got a C in maths and my science teacher said I am showing potential in chemistry. Plus, I love ice-skating. I never go ice-skating, but maybe that's my talent? Or running or writing or teaching or mechanics. Or maybe I hadn't found my talent yet because I'm only 13! Mum releases me from her clutches as I tried to wipe the stain of her hugs off me and I asked,

"Is kindness actually a talent?" Because I thought a talent is being good at art or dancing or science but she grabbed me again and hugged me more saying,

"You're my good, kind girl."

"Please stop squeezing me!" I say.

"Why can't I hug my baby?" she says as she lets me go.

"You're leaving your stain on me!"

"A stain???! Hugs are a lovely thing M! It should leave you with a nice warm glow! Why do you say such horrid things?"

Oh no! I think I've hurt her again. She turns away from me and adds Toby's latest achievement to the layers of his certificates on the fridge door and she says,

"It's just a hug for God's sake!"

I went up to my room to watch Skylar, season 3, episode 4. The one in which she wears lilac ballet pumps, navy blue skinny jeans and silver heart earrings and she goes on a spa weekend with her mom but she discovers a money laundering business in the basement of this big hotel. Skylar and her mom hug loads in this episode. I wish I liked hugs.

Tuesday 4.00pm

I wanted to talk about so much! I wanted to talk about this new boy in the year above me at school called Lynx. I want to talk about being given "extra support" at school but I also wanted to talk about hugs and upsetting my mum too and how I was angry about being a kind girl but now all I feel is guilty. The counsellor said,

"Let's start with you being called kind. What does it feel like when your mum tells you your talent is kindness?" I explained that sometimes I liked it because I think she means it to be a nice thing but something isn't right too because Toby isn't called kind. He is called clever, the best, the most successful. So why are we different? Is it because he's a boy?

"Is it enough for you M? Is it enough to be a kind, good girl?"

"I am kind and I like being kind," I reply. "Sometimes I don't think Mum knows what to do with me. Or what to call me. She knows I'm different and I know I'm different and I think she just finds it easy to call me kind."

COUNSELLOR SILENCE

And then she asked again,

"But is it enough for you M? In your life. Is it enough for you to be a good, kind girl?"

"No," I said.

"What do you want to do with your life?"

"I want to be an artist or work with animals or be a human rights activist or maybe an ice-skater."

That's what I want.

I want a job.

I want training.

I want qualifications.

I think I am clever. I just get the anxiety and it stops me, especially since I've started at St Andrews secondary school. I can't even walk into some classrooms, like K3 and K4 in the B Block.

They have so much echo and then there are the buzzing lights in Room B8 and B2, and all the doors in the maths departments really BANG loudly when they shut. So how can I learn when I can't even walk into some classrooms?

I just want to be normal, like the others, and just walk into a room and learn and not care about a scraping chair, a slamming door or worry about the paint peeling from the ceiling in the English rooms. I feel the tears well up in my eyes and just the thought of it makes me feel anxious.

"Take some deep breaths," instructs Fiona, and I do. "I understand," she continues. "I understand 100 per cent." And I believe her. I really think she might be the only person who does and that feels good.

"What is the latest feedback from your doctor and the hospital?" she asks.

"I've got lots of appointments," I say. "Lots of forms to fill in, so they can find out what's wrong with me. Someone says I am OCD, another doctor thinks I'm autistic and someone else just thinks I've got lots of wax in my ears and that's the reason I don't answer in class."

"I don't think it's wax in your ears M. Maybe you are on the autistic spectrum or maybe you have OCD too but you need to get a diagnosis from a specialist and find out.

You're clearly a clever girl M and judging by your school reports you can achieve good qualifications, you just need some more support at school. So you can have a career AND be kind. It's not one or the other."

I nod. This is good to hear.

"You are dealing with so much," says Fiona.

"Yes," I say. "I am and I'm very, very tired."

Trying to fit in and be normal and put on my mask every day is very tiring...plus being in love with Lynx makes life exhausting.

Chapter 3

M said she thinks we live in an overpopulated planet and she doesn't think there's enough room for her. A mother doesn't want to hear her daughter say this...

Dave never understood M. He would get impatient at her being quiet and was always criticising her anxieties. He was always stressed and anxious too, so you'd think he would understand his own daughter. They are very similar and I used to tell him,

"She gets it from you Dave!"

And then we'd row and well, the strain became impossible, so, after years of trying, he moved out. He moved up to London and we still see him and of course I miss him terribly, but to be honest the pressure at home eased a lot but it wasn't what I wanted. I wanted a normal family.

So here I am on a Friday night making fajitas for M and me...it's her favourite. It's one of the only things she will eat. She's a fussy eater and this used to wind up Dave too. He'd shout,

"Why can't she just fit in and eat the same as us?!"

M would cry and shake and every mealtime descended into a family row; at least that's stopped now. So here I am chopping onions and trying to bond with my beautiful daughter but it's not easy. It should be, shouldn't it? But reaching her and connecting with her feels so hopeless, so futile, but today I am making a big effort. I am her mother and I cannot give up on her or let her down.

I'm really trying.

Every day I think, today's the day she'll tell me about school and her friends and if there are any boys she likes and I can advise her and we can have a giggle. Mother and daughter having a proper heart to heart. Just as I'm grating the cheese M comes in,

"Hi M! How are you my darling?" She goes straight to the dog for a cuddle. I ask her about her day.

One-word response.

I suggest we go shopping on Saturday. M loves clothes.

Blank face.

"Are you being all dolly daydream?" I ask. M takes herself off into her own little world sometimes. She's told her grandma once about a crystal lake and generations of owl families in a faraway mountain. She never shared it with me...that hurt. I do like that she has this imagination but it worries me too that she uses it to cut herself off from us. Dave found out about her fantasy world and hated it. He used to shout at her and tell her to,

"Stop with all this willful madness."

But you know I think this made M more stressed and retreat from us even more. In fact she told Grandma that she'd created an even bigger world with more forests and more crystal lakes, to escape into. I didn't mention it to Dave.

But back to our mother and daughter Friday night... M starts to go upstairs. This isn't going well.

"Wait M!" I call. Reluctantly, she stops and turns.

"What are you making?" she asks. Great! She's talking to me! She's engaging.

"Fajitas!" I say in a Mexican accent, hoping I'll make her giggle. She doesn't giggle. She never giggles. I want to shout, "Lighten up girl!" But I bite my tongue. Experience has taught me that never goes down well.

"You said we were having pizza and chips." She's right, that was the plan and I have changed the plan. The truth is I forgot and I know how much she hates change. How could I forget? Sometimes I think I'll get an award, like Toby's, but it will be for "World's Most Rubbish Mother."

"Sorry honey! I was so busy and I...but you like fajitas, don't you?"

"It's just you said pizza and chips Mum,"

"I'll make it up to you," I reply but really I want to say, "Be more flexible lady! Cause it's a tough old world out there and fajitas will be the least of your problems in a few years when you have to pay bills and get a mortgage!" But I know that will make things worse. She keeps cuddling the dog. I am so jealous of the dog. Deep breath. I read my fridge magnet, "Practise compassion and you practise love." I try again.

"We should go and see Grandma on Sunday and help her with the garden. You love her garden, don't you?"

She looks up briefly and says, "Yes." But not a lot more is said.

I chop peppers, seething. That dog gets hugs that should be for me. Her mum. I feel robbed of a daughter and then I feel so sad that we are unable to chat, then frustration creeps in and the tension rises between us both as she disappears upstairs... I let her go this time.

My "mum" friends say this is a typical mother and daughter conversation and I'm not to worry and they kindly share an example of their disagreements, but M is not the same as their daughters. She's never been the same... Friends say she'll get over it. You see that's part of the problem...she never seems to just "get over" things. I think I am beginning to realise that maybe she can't...

Chapter 4

"The noise feels like someone has a knife and has sliced off the top of my head, exposing my brain, which feels like a balloon, ready to burst."

Joe and I were sitting at our desks waiting for registration. Miss Green is often late. 8.46 or 8.47 or 8.52, even 9.02. She says that sometimes she has to help at the school gates but still, it's difficult for me. She's told me not to be so sensitive and I should be used to it by now. Why should I get used to her being late?

Should	[aux.v. Past tense of shall]
	1. Used to express obligation or duty: "You should send her a note."
	2. Used to express probability or expectation: "They should arrive at noon."

But just because Miss Green is repeatedly late it doesn't make it any easier for me to deal with. It doesn't mean I get used to it. It just means I know how anxious I will get and how bad my anxiety will be. So in fact it's worse!

As always, I can sense anxiety prowling outside the classroom. It's outside the window. Looking in at me.

Registration is at 8.45. That is what it states on the school website. That's what it says on the school noticeboard. Miss Green said I need to understand that sometimes she gets caught up with incidents or meetings but registration is at 8.45. Miss Green should [aux.v. Past tense of shall] be here at 8.45.

Joe sits next to me in form time. This morning he asked me if I'd watched Claw Hand on YouTube. I told him Toby was watching Claw Hand but I was watching Skylar. Sometimes I find it easier to talk to boys than girls. I find boys straightforward. They just ask a question and I answer it. I ask a question and they answer it. Joe said he liked my hair clip and asked where I got it,

"Off the internet," I said. "It's called Tangerine Dream. I really like the flecks of silver and it's like Skylar's hair grip in season 4, episode 2. In the scene where she finds that the school secretary has been spending the school funds on a limousine and manicures." He laughs.

"It's not funny Joe! She was arrested for embezzlement and went to Penn State Correctional Institution for 2 years. She was stealing."

"You just make me laugh sometimes M." Sometimes I really don't understand why people laugh. Sometimes I laugh along with them, to fit in. "Your hair grip, it's pretty," he adds.

"Yes, I know it is," I reply and my reply makes him laugh again. Then he asks me more about Skylar.

"It's the best TV programme ever. She is so cool and she has so many friends and she's this all-American girl..."

"Is that why you talk in an American accent sometimes?" he interrupts. I pretend not to hear and keep talking. The truth is I do pick up sounds and accents. I remember tones and intonations (my counsellor says I am receptive and sensitive). But the truth is sometimes I find it easier to be someone else. Anyway, I tell Joe more about Skylar and how she is really beautiful. She is 17 or 18 and solves lots of mysteries while wearing really fashionable clothes, and then the show always ends with Skylar performing a song in a high school hall or at a really cool festival. Joe was really listening and I was thinking this was great. Me and Joe were having a normal conversation. Like normal people. I can be normal. I like being normal.

Then Shaznia **BURSTS** through the door screaming, clutching a handful of invitations and my world shifts from "an attempt at being normal" to "hell." My world melts and I am terrified. Along with Shaznia, anxiety has crashed into the room and jumped on my back and is ripping at my throat and my nerves.

Everyone jumps off their desks and seats and tries to grab the envelopes out of Shaznia's hand. The decibels in the room rise and the noise is like screeching brakes! Sirens! Alarms!

And all so sudden and shrill! A sharp pain stabs in my ears.

Everyone wanted to go to this party and everyone's been talking about it. It's going to be a really awesome party. But the screeching and the shouting made it impossible for me to be happy about it, even though I really wanted to go! I put my hands over my ears. And now a huge part of me really doesn't want to go but I know Lynx will be there. Lynx.

Beautiful, scented, hair gelled, sparkly eyed, calm, kind, intelligent, softly spoken, juicy lipped, pop star style, tall, smiling love of my life Lynx.

I love Lynx. I really, really love him.

I watched from the edge of my seat as they scrambled for invitations and scrabbled about on the floor as some of them fell from Shaznia's hand and she handed the rest out.

Where was my invitation?

Jade was squealing.

Ben said he'd try and make it but he might be at another party that night.

Charlotte told everyone she was going to spray glitter in her hair.

Where was my invitation?

Nev and Lara were planning to meet at the park first.

Joe didn't open his. He just put it in his blazer pocket and told me he'd only go if I was going.

Where was mine?

Jade asked if she could bring some drink.

Lainey asked what I was wearing. I was finding it hard to breath. Shaznia had said she was going to give me an invitation but where was it? I tapped my cheeks with my fingers.

"I d-don't have an i-i-invitation," I stuttered. I could feel my face burning and I knew my cheeks would be bright red.

"Shaznia mustn't like you anymore," Lara said. Then Nev added,

"Shaz only wants pretty girls at the party." The whole class's attention turned to me. So many eyes, staring at me.

"Hey!" cried out Nev in an American accent. "Maybe M will wear a prom dress!" And a few people giggled.

"Shut up!" I said, as tears welled up in my eyes. I tried to stop them but I felt like my head might explode.

"Maybe Shaz doesn't like your bad attitude," taunted Nev. Lara laughed and said,

"M hardly talks and when she does it's sooo rude. You need to show some manners girl!" And anxiety tore at my nerves and I felt like I was going crazy. It wasn't fair! And I HIT my hand on the desk. I banged my hand so hard that a sharp, stinging pain shot through my wrist. My head was so fuzzy and I saw everyone backing off a little, but their eyes were still on me.

"OK, crazy girl," says Nev, "it's a joke. We are joking. Are you too stupid to get a joke?"

"I'm sure I wrote you an invitation M," said Shaznia and she looked about under desks and chairs.

"She's a freak. She should be locked up in a mental house," said Lara.

"She's upset, can't you see that?" shouted Joe.

"Just cause you fancy M," Nev said, and Joe backed off.

I wanted to be somewhere else. I want to bolt but the classroom door was too far away...

So I started to think about MOLW and a unicorn leaps through my mind and leads me to the Lake of Calm. A gentle pink mist hovers over the still water. Trees with generations of owl families hoot gently, nesting in the branches of the friendly forest and amongst a hedgerow sweet, little mice play. I spot a gate covered in tangled ivy for me to open and explore a whole new and precious land. An owl swoops down and rests on my shoulder. My feathered friend to accompany me on my happy journey.

Then CUT right through the pink mist I saw an envelope with M printed on it. Joe was holding it, right up to my face.

"It fell on the floor," said Joe. "You are invited."

"Of course you're invited," said Shaznia, "I wasn't going to leave you out, was I? It fell under a chair."

Then Miss Green blustered in, all bothered and stressy, with a pile of exercise books spewing out from her arms, whilst clutching a mug of coffee and everyone went back to their desks.

"Sorry 8G. I was caught up in an incident at the school gates and it's assessments this week so I've got all this marking and it's been a very, very stressful morning for me."

It was 8.56. Maybe she shouldn't have got that mug of coffee because if she'd arrived at 8.45 my wrist wouldn't be hurting. She should have arrived at 8.45 because my life was in shreds and I didn't know how I could make it through the day.

"Are you OK?" whispered Joe.

"I'm fine," I lied.

"Do you think you'll go to the party?" he asked. I so wanted to go. I really, really, really wanted to go. I desperately wanted to go, I knew Lynx will be there. The florescent light in the classroom buzzed and flashed in my eyes and made me feel nauseous. I held my painful wrist and the beast of anxiety continued to prowl round the room, it's threatening, fixed stare boring into me.

"Maybe we could meet first? Go in together?"

"I'm not sure I'm able to," I replied.

Chapter 5

"Something is not as
it should be."

When **M** was a baby I had a group of friends and we'd take it in turns to have tea, coffee and cakes together giving our babies the opportunity to interact, learn to share and socialise, etc... In the back of my head I had niggles that my baby daughter was different to Toby but then Toby is a boisterous, outgoing boy so I tried to rationalise my fears and think, "They're just different characters!" but I couldn't deny it any longer, my precious baby wasn't like the others at our coffee mornings.

I watched as she genuinely struggled with joining in. She just wanted to be in her own little world. Other children would try and socialise with her and I would encourage her to play with them, but I could see this made her so anxious. She wouldn't share her toys. I felt embarrassed. Even when I tried to explain to her or swap her toy for a cake or another toy she just would not share. I couldn't get her to play with anything but her plastic bricks. They were all she was interested in. She was obsessive with them.

I knew my baby didn't interact like others and then I had to find out why.

Doctors' appointments.

Wait and see...monitor behaviour.

Fill in this form.

Fill in that form.

Counsellor's appointments.

Educational psychologist.

She'll grow out of it. Stop fussing.

All I want is for someone to listen to me, to understand that something is not as it should be. I am the parent, I know my child.

Back to the doctor.

Referrals.

All I wanted was a normal family life.

Hospital appointment.

Health visitor.

The ear specialist, "Maybe she's just hard of hearing. Too much wax, bunging her up! She's not ignoring you!"

Hearing test.

Back to the doctor.

Psychiatrist.

Do any of these people talk to each other?

Ears are fine.

Could be multiple complex needs.

Asperger's, dyslexia, dyspraxia, anxiety issues, panic attacks, autism, OCD, ADHD, agoraphobia, borderline personality disorder, depression (clinical), depression (low mood), dissociative disorders, personality disorder, post-traumatic stress disorder, psychosis, schizophrenia, seasonal affective disorder (SAD), stress? Stress?
Child and Adolescent Mental Health Services

"I think it's autism," I say to the specialist, teachers and psychologists, but no one listens... "I've had a look on the internet and..."

"Oh! You're an internet doctor are you?"

Fill in another form.

Have you thought about seeing a counsellor?

My daughter already sees a counsellor.

Not her. You.

Why? Do you think I am imagining this?

Back to the doctor.

And everything revolves around money, lack of professionals and facilities, being pushed from one professional to another, appointment after appointment after appointment after appointment. Are they frightened that I will yell and shout if I'm told that my daughter is autistic, Asperger, OCD, personality disorder or whatever? No one will commit!

I just want to know what's wrong with my baby!

I just want to know why she behaves like she does, why she won't connect with me, why she's so anxious. Maybe there's a cure for her? If I know, then I will be in a stronger place to help her, support her and to understand her. I NEED to know!

Chapter 6

It's a jumbled up world. A tangled up, rough and bumpy place to live. With strong, smooth edges and a sour, hot, bitter taste.

"Dance! **M** dance!" I was finding the instruction to dance difficult so I just stood against the damp, hard wall of the local church hall. The tall ceiling meant the noise was traveling round the room and the music sounded really big and wide and very loud. The DJ was telling everyone to shout out and everyone's whoops and shouts flew up into the ceiling and crashed around, echoing and then bounced down into my head. The sounds were filling the hall and battling with all the multi-coloured lights – flashing and twisting and swirling! I could feel a sharp pain in the side of my brain and my wrist was still aching from a couple of weeks ago when I banged it on the desk. Oh why did I come? So many people and new people. Faces I didn't recognise. I didn't know there would be new people. I don't like new people. They are unknowns. Who are they and what do they want? And what was I doing here? Really? What was I thinking? But I wanted to see if Lynx would be here and I kept scanning the room for him. Would he turn up?

And I want to have friends. I desperately want friends and I want to do what the normal girls do. I just want to fit in.

I had looked at myself in the mirror, before I left my bedroom, and said,

"I'm not going to ruin this! I'm not going to let myself get the better of me. I am going to make friends. I want to see Lynx! Tonight, **M** is going to be **A***."

But already I felt the evening slipping to an F minus as I noticed Nev and Lara and hoped they'd stay on the other side of the hall. Joe appeared and stood next to me and said I looked nice and asked if I'd watched Claw Hand yet. I hadn't. I asked if he'd watched Skylar and he hadn't. He asked about the art homework and said he thought my work was really good and he asked if I was going on the school trip to Paris.

"No," I replied. The idea of travelling to France on a coach and a boat was out of the question.

"That's a shame," he answered. He's right. It is a shame and it's unfair that I can't do what everyone else in my class can do. The normal people.

"Why can't you come M? It's going to be really cool."

"I'm staying with my dad that weekend," I lied, adding to my shame.

"Would you like another coke?" he asked.

"What?" The loud music was making it really hard to focus and listen. Anxiety had been creeping up my arms and legs all day and was now beginning to crawl towards my throat, distracting me from normal life, again.

"Can I get you another drink M?" repeated Joe, shouting this time. I flinched.

"Why would I want another drink?" I replied. "Can't you see I have a full glass?"

"OK M," he replied, "there's no need to be rude. I was trying to be friendly." Rude? I wasn't being rude. It's just I didn't need another drink. Had I upset Joe? Oh no! I'd just answered his question with the correct information. Oh, I didn't want to upset Joe.

"Joe!" shouted Jade from the dance floor. "Come and dance!" Her shout cut through me and I tensed up.

"Ermmm, M, will you come and dance too?" I said no. I was finding this hard. I kept messing up and all the noise. I was yearning to be invisible, to have no face, no body. **No face**.

I felt pointless. Joe went to dance and said he'd be back in 5 minutes. I did want to dance but it just wasn't possible.

How come everyone loves loud music so much? Why don't I? Why can't I be normal and enjoy what all the other girls love? What makes the normal girls so excited and hyped up, in a good way? Not in an anxious, stressed, terrified way, like me? What makes us so different?

"Come on M! Dance!" shouted Shaznia but I felt sick. I so wanted to be normal and do what all the normal girls do. That's why I went. I just wanted to fit in.

The normal girls, they know what to do. They get things right.

I was feeling sick. What if I *got* sick?

"What a pretty skirt!" said Shaznia's mum as she passed with a tray of cakes. I was wearing the same outfit as Skylar, in the final scene of season 3, episode 7. Lots of people say I dress nicely but mostly I just copy Skylar. Then a song from Skylar came on. It was my favourite song from all the episodes but this was different. A remix. It had been changed. Why? Why would they change the song?

"Are you OK?" asked Shaznia's mum.

"She's the quiet one. She's called M," said another adult, passing by with a black bin liner which crinkled noisily as she shoved in empty plastic cups and plates. "Why don't you let yourself go? Have a dance with all the other girls? It's silly you standing here on your own. You need to be braver. Pull yourself together and get out there on the dance floor. I'm just giving you good advice from the heart, darling. Sometimes in life you need to let go."

Need? Is that what I *need* to do to be normal?

"You look frightened, love," said Shaznia's mum and the Bin Liner lady continued to ram polystyrene plates in the plastic bag, scraping and cracking and ripping my ears and asked,

"Is that the girl they think might have Asper...or what's the other one? Autistic? Is she the one who's always off school, at the hospital? It's the disease where you get obsessed with numbers and they say lots of criminals have it? It is, isn't it? Dyslexia? Or autism or the other one?"

Adults do this. Doctors do this. Teachers do this. Neighbours do this. Mum's friends, they talk about me as if I can't hear.

Then a scent filled my whole olfactory system! A scent of joy and ecstasy. Better than crystal lakes and Skylar. Better than the flowers in Grandma's garden or fajitas.

Lynx entered the church hall.

I swear St Mark's Church hall became heaven. I wasn't sure I could keep breathing if I kept looking at him, so I just looked down at my pretty, lilac stilettos. From the corner of my eye I could see him walk towards me! I could smell his aftershave stronger and stronger! What if he talked to me!? What would I say? I watched his feet as they walked past mine, and I smelt this powerful scent as he wafted past me to the drinks table.

He smelt of being grown up and normal or maybe this is what it is like being drunk. I'd been to Superdrug and smelt all the different Lynx scents. Amber, Cedarwood, Ibiza, Temptation, Excite, Peace, Apollo, Africa and all the specials in the Christmas range. I knew them all and he was wearing Cedarwood. Heavenly. Sublime. Divine. Ecstasy.

But I was on overload and I felt a fool as I saw Lynx talking to Charlotte. Did he love her? And I looked at the church hall clock and it had been 5 minutes and Joe had not returned, as he said he would. Why did he say 5 minutes when he didn't mean it? All my senses were on one million per cent. Anxiety had me in a headlock and its gnarly hand was inside my throat! I couldn't breathe. I was being violently shaken and I felt like I would faint or scream. Was I being crushed to death? And I saw the pink mist roll out in front of me. MOLW, so inviting, so safe but I could also see the green light of the EXIT sign of the church hall shining through, so I bolted. My clicky, pretty, lilac stilettos clicked all the way home as I was chased, relentlessly, by the frightening wild animal that held no compassion for me.

The beast that will never reason with me, just picks on me at its will. Like I'm some kind of sport or prey it is entitled to.

Finally I made it home and I banged repeatedly on the front door.

bang bang bang bang bang bang bang bang bang bang bang bang bang bang bang bang bang bang

Mum opened the door and drained of energy I entered and sank down to the rough carpet and gasped for breath. Mum grabbed me and tried to pick me up, while bombarding me with questions.

"M! Are you all right? What's wrong? Is someone chasing you?" She let me go and ran up the front garden path to see if I'd been followed home and I scrunched myself up into a little ball, and I could hardly breathe.

65

I was fighting to get oxygen into my lungs.

The dog ran into the hall barking and still I heard Mum asking questions.

"M, are you alone? M please!!! What's happened?" I couldn't take this pressure. So I charged up the stairs and disappeared into my room. I looked at myself in the mirror and I desperately wanted to scream! But I couldn't. Nothing inside me would budge. I wanted to scream the beast out of me.

I just wanted to be normal!

I looked at my dishevelled reflection and felt so frustrated that tonight was not an **A***. It was **Z**.

Z. A rubbish, horrible, nasty, no-good Z and I looked down at my pretty, lilac stilettos. They were scuffed, ruined.

The front doorbell rang. I heard Mum answer and then I heard Joe's voice and him asking if I was OK and mum was asking him what happened. They both knocked on my bedroom door but I really wanted to be alone and I told them to go away.

I put on season 2, episode 9 of Skylar...the one where she goes to a prom and everyone turns into zombies and she's wearing sky-blue ankle socks and grey patent ballet pumps.

Tuesday 4.00pm

Next time I see the counsellor, I tell her all about the disco and the anxiety and the overload and how awful it all was. She said she was so sorry to hear that and she agreed it must have been awful. I even begin to feel anxious thinking about it and I beat my fingers on my cheeks.

"Stop a moment M," says Fiona. "Close your eyes and take some deep breaths." And I do. "Focus on your breathing," she continues. "In 1, 2, 3, 4 and slowly breath out..." And after a while I open my eyes and still feel an edge of anxiety but the beast is much further away than usual...

And do you know what Fiona said then? She said,

"I think you did incredibly well M." She actually said she was proud of me for going to the disco and trying so hard to do something I really wanted to do. So I told her about Lynx and his intoxicating scent and me dressing like Skylar, season 2, episode 9. I told her about my anxiety levels and she said she was going to talk to my mum about speeding up my diagnosis at the hospital.

"I really think you are showing signs of autism M." My mum has been saying this for ages now.

"Is that what's wrong with me?"

"Let me make it very clear M and I want you to really take this is in – there is nothing wrong with you."

COUNSELLOR SILENCE

Then she continued, "I just think you process information in a very certain way."

"Differently?" I question.

"Well," she replied, "different to some people."

"Different to the people at school?"

"Maybe," she replied.

"We need a doctor to confirm a diagnosis for you and make it official."

"Official?" I repeat and I am not sure I like this. "Am I going to be labelled? Who will that help?" I ask.

"You," she replies.

"Will I ever be normal?" I ask.

"What is normal?"

She answers my question with a question so I work out my own answer...

So I think and say...

"I think it's having friends and maybe talking to boys. Being like Shaznia.

Being able to chat. I can't chat. Will there be a cure for me? So I can be normal?"

"M I'd like to see you in a more supportive school or getting some extra tuition. It's good that we talk about your feelings but I want to see more practical support put in place for you. I think you're struggling too much. Everyone has a bad day, week, month even year but this is too much M. This is constant stress and anxiety. Life shouldn't be too much of a struggle M."

She's right. Less of a struggle would be good. Life is a struggle when you're trying to be normal.

Chapter 7

Time is my enemy.
I am stuck in time.

It traps me.

I have no sense of time.

It's **Wednesday** 19th June and it is **8.46** in the morning. Mum said we would leave at **8.45** for, as she says, "possibly the most important day of our lives." She is already late for my diagnosis day at the hospital. I am wearing a mint green T-shirt dress, a denim jacket and I am carrying a small, tan leather handbag, with matching lace-up Oxfords. It's the outfit Skylar wears in season 4, episode 3, when she flew to New York City to visit her long-lost aunt. The thought of the whole day ahead was making me anxious. ANXIOUS. Trains, buses, appointments. Mum had written me a list of the day's events:

8.45	meet in the hall to leave the house.
9.00	catch the 184, 263 or 348 bus to station.
9.16	train to city centre.
9.50	alight train.
10.00	have a Frappuccino in a coffee shop near the hospital, so I can have a breather and prepare for the appointment.
10.30	appointment.

It was now **8.47**.

8.47 I hugged the dog and tried to calm myself.

8.48 I called up the stairs, "Mum!"

8.49 "OK! OK!" she says as she clumps, loudly, down the stairs, clutching the hospital letter and we shut the front door behind us. She is wearing pink lipstick and smells of Blue Rose perfume. Mum wearing perfume confirms the importance of the day.

"This could be a really great day for us M, and don't you look so beautiful in your blue dress."

"It's mint green."

"Oh M, I'm giving you a compliment! Accept it for God's sake!" But how can I accept a compliment? She hasn't given me the correct information.

"But it's green, Mum! Mint green!" And I think I'm going to faint as anxiety rears its head and scrapes at my skin as we head towards the bus stop.

"Can we NOT have an argument?" she shouts. "This could be the best day of our lives."

But it's already feeling like an F day and as we rush for the bus all I can think about is getting my aisle seat on the bus and Mum shouting at me about my dress when she got the colour wrong.

We run for the bus, anxiety pacing menacingly alongside me the whole time, watching me, and when the doors of the bus screech and bang open I can't get on because anxiety won't let me. The bus driver waits. Anxiety's dead weight has jumped on my back and is holding me down. I can't take a step on to the bus. Why did Mum write me a list and then change the times? And I hate hospitals. Bad things happen in hospitals. I don't want to go and find out bad things.

"M, come on sweetheart. Just step up on the bus. This is our important day."

"I know, I know!" I want to shout but I don't say anything. Instead I flap my hands and I can feel my throat narrowing with fear. All the passengers are staring at me and I feel their disapproval and annoyance.

"Come on M, put one foot on the step. It's easy!" The engine is **ROARING** and the bus feels so **HOT** on my cheeks and I want an aisle seat and I can't see one that's free and it's just not that easy. If it was easy I'd get on the bus! Cars are lining up behind the bus and a driver is beeping his horn repeatedly and a passenger loses her patience and shouts,

"Some of us have got to get to work you know!"

"I can't wait for you any longer love, I'll get the sack," adds the bus driver.

"Can we get the next bus Mum?" I ask. "Please?" Mum sighs.

"OK." And reluctantly she steps off the number 26 and shouts out an apology to all the passengers. "She's a bit stressed. She's not feeling well today!" Anxiety snarls at me. It has bullied me into submission again. There's an awkward silence as we wait for the next bus. Mum is angry. I'll be more prepared for the next bus. I've got my pass in my left hand. I will hold the rail with my right hand as I enter the bus and hopefully I'll get an aisle seat. What if there isn't an aisle seat? My throat gets tighter and I want to cry. Mum breaks the silence and snaps,

"This is a very important day M. This could be the most important day of our lives."

I know this and that is why I feel so very, very anxious.

We spin through a revolving door, take a dark lift to the 7th floor and walk down antiseptic corridors and into the doctor's white room. The bright florescent lights hit my eyes and my head pounds, harder. A wall clock ticks. **10.40.** We didn't have time for the planned Frappuccino, for me to have a breather before the appointment.

"Sorry we're late!" apologises Mum.

"Is that quite stressful for you M, when you are late?" Not QUITE stressful, I want to shout. It's terrifying. TERRIFYING but I don't say anything. The light is buzzing in my ears too. My whole brain is buzzing.

"Sorry she doesn't say much," says Mum, apologising for me, for the third time that day. I think I must really embarrass Mum a lot.

"This shouldn't take long," says the doctor, "a few minutes." And they talk for 10 minutes.

10.50.

Mum fills in more forms and then the doctor turns to me and asks me lots of questions.

11.10. The doctor said a few minutes. What exactly is a few minutes? How long is that?

The doctor fills in lots of forms and taps in lots of words to the computer and Mum and I sit and wait.

BUZZZZZZZZZZZZZZZZZ.

Waiting.

BUZZZZZZZZZZZZZZZZZZ.

What is the doctor going to say? Oh God, what will they find wrong with me? And it's **11.20**. Mum thinks it's going to be autism but what if it's something else? What if they send me to a hospital and I have to stay there? Mum senses my anxiety and smiles at me. She goes to squeeze my hand and I pull it away. I don't want to be squeezed. I want to ask how much longer all this will take. But I can't speak.

At **11.36** the doctor stops typing and turns to me and my mum. She says that she will be diagnosing me with autism. Mum breathes a huge sigh and repeats,

"Autism?"

"Yes," Confirms the doctor.

It's **11.36** and I have autism.

"I knew it," says Mum. "I was so sure that's what she has. It's just so good that it's official. Thank you, Doctor. Thank you so much."

"And we'll be sending a letter in the post to confirm the diagnosis."

JUST LIKE THAT. DIAGNOSED.

And we walk back through antiseptic corridors, take a dark lift down to ground level, we spin through the revolving doors and I'm spat out on the street.

I AM AUTISTIC.

What the hell does that mean?

On the bus back to our house I was sitting on the aisle seat as Mum was busy texting everyone. I've never seen Mum so happy. She was happier than when Toby gets a certificate.

"GOT DIAGNOSIS – AUTISM!" she texted Grandma and Granddad.

"SO HAPPY YOU'VE GOT AN ANSWER TO EVERYTHING," replied Grandma. Then she texted her Mum friend, Jacky.

"I WAS RIGHT JACKS, M's GOT AUTISM," Jacky promptly replies,

"STAY STRONG. I AM PLEASED FOR YOU. LIFE WILL START TO GET BETTER XXXXXX"

My diagnosis seemed to be making people happy. Until she texted my dad, who replied,

"OK. THANK YOU FOR LETTING ME KNOW. TELL M IT'S NOT AN EXCUSE FOR BAD BEHAVIOUR."

I could see big, fat tears fall from her eyes. Those really sad tears. She wiped the condensation off the bus window with her jacket sleeve and really angrily she said,

"These bus windows are so dirty. I don't understand him. He's meant to care. He's your father. I can hardly make out anything through this stupid window. Is that a tree or a lamp post? How the hell are you supposed to know where you are or where you're going? God, this is all so frustrating!"

I just sit beside her and think, that's how I feel all the time.

Tuesday 4.00pm

"I think this is very good news," says Fiona when I tell her. "Do you think it's good news M?" she asks.

"I think so," I reply. "But no as well. I looked autism up in the dictionary when I got home and it said I was a failure and it's boys who have autism. It said:

Autism [noun]	
	A failure to develop social abilities, language, and other communication skills to the usual level: Autism is four times more common in boys than in girls.

"Let me tell you right now M, that's a dictionary definition written by someone in an office years ago, who sounds very out of touch and insensitive. You define it for me."

So I thought and said,

"It's a frightening world, it's tipsy, turvy and wobbly. It's lonely and full on and sometimes it's volcanic. But it's my world and I can communicate. Sometimes people just need to listen to me or wait but what about it being for boys? Now I feel even weirder. Like I am weird in an already different world."

"More boys get a diagnosis. People think it's a 'boy's condition' but it's not M. That's an outdated view. More and more girls are being diagnosed with autism."

COUNSELLOR SILENCE

"I think this diagnosis will help you because just being able to understand yourself a little more will give you more control in your life."

"I thought they might give me tablets to be normal. Will they find a cure one day?"

"There are no tablets to make you 'not autistic' because there isn't anything wrong with you."

"But I'm autistic and they told me that at a hospital, where sick people go, so I must have an illness. That's my diagnosis. My illness. My sickness. It's logical."

COUNSELLOR SILENCE

"It's not an illness. It's more a way of being. It's your wonderful state of mind, the way you view the world. That's not being ill."

"But I'm not normal. How do I change and get better and get normal?"

"Why should you change?" asks Fiona. "There's nothing wrong with you M." And I find it so hard to understand what Fiona means because my whole life I've been told I'm not normal and that there is a problem with me and something isn't quite right.

COUNSELLOR
SILENCE

"Did the hospital refer you to a specialist or tell you about a special school or getting a qualified support worker for you in the classroom? Did anyone at the hospital say what would happen next?" she asks.

"No," I reply. "No one's said anything. I don't know what happens next. I feel like I've been dropped into a big abyss and I'm free falling but then it does also feel like the beginning of something. I'm just not sure what it is or what to do about being autistic."

"And you or your mum can't possibly have all the answers and there will probably be trial and error in some of your decisions, but I really believe this is a very positive thing. I think it will help you find your feet in life."

"Find my feet?"

"Feel more secure in life."

Our hour is up and I leave Fiona's powder blue room feeling hot and I can feel my anxiety rising. I usually leave Fiona's room feeling OK but today I feel anxiety screeching "trial and error" in my ears.

Trial and error going round and round my head.

"Trial and error" doesn't feel like a very positive thing but I do like the idea of finding my feet.

Chapter 8

At least my own little world remains the same, but as for the one I have to share with everyone else, well I guess it will keep turning and changing and I'll keep trying to cling on.

A few weeks after the diagnosis a letter arrived.

A list of conditions and further investigations of the assessment
criteria. Monitoring and regulations of issues and the primary
resource and skills-based systems and prognosis.

And that after routine tests and assessment by the Mental Health
and Educational Learning Team at St James's your daughter has a
diagnosis of Autism.

It was the summer holidays and Mum was in the garden
all the time, digging, cutting things back and chatting
with the neighbours over the fence. She left the letter
on the kitchen table under a glass vase of yellow roses.
Mum was doing nice things since the diagnosis: buying
flowers, baking cakes, writing poems, gardening again
and wearing Blue Rose perfume, even when it's not a
special occasion.

For me, life was the same really. I like the summer holidays
and not having to get on buses and deal with late teachers
at school. I really missed seeing Lynx though. But the
angry beast never goes on holiday. It still prowls round
and intimidates me. When I go shopping it still roars in
my ear or lurks in supermarket aisles and outside the
kitchen window.

But back to the letter, it just made being autistic all more
official really. Seeing my name and the word autistic typed
on the hospital headed paper meant it was definite. Mum
was reading loads of stuff on the internet and printing
reams of pages off about autism and leaving them on my
bed to read. Pages with titles like:

Autism and your child

CAMHS and how we can help

Autism and your future

Autism – is it just boys?

Autism and the family: how to cope

The way I felt in life was making a little bit more sense and I could also see that I wasn't the only person in the world who felt like this.

One evening Mum sat me and Toby down. She only does this when she has something important to say like when her and Dad split up or when Granddad died. I felt very anxious as she took her gardening gloves off and poured us all some homemade lemonade.

"Your father and I have been talking," Toby raised his eyes to heaven. "There's a school in London," Mum continued. "It's especially for children with autism and your father and I were thinking, you know, about you going there M."

My head juddered.

"And, you know, staying with Dad in the week," she added.

The beast was in the room and snorting. Staring at me. Had my parents gone completely mad? Just when I thought things were getting a "little bit" better. Hadn't she read any of the pages she left on the bed about people with autism not liking change????? I tapped my cheeks with my fingers. Surely Mum would now *see* I was getting stressed? Surely she would stop talking about a new school and a new place to live?

"Look, we have to get this *thing* called a Statement, which means you are entitled to lots of things."

"Things??" I repeat. "What things?" I said. I didn't understand what THINGS were. One of the printouts mum left me said "be very clear when talking to someone with autism." So I told her,

"Be clear Mum. Be very clear. What are *things*?" She looked shocked at me and she drank some lemonade.

"Ermmm... Gosh M, things like, going to a special school and apparently they are really difficult to get into but the psychiatrist at the hospital said we are entitled to one... so we *will* get one... A Statement, that is."

"We? Are we all going to the special school?" I ask.

"Don't be stupid!" shouted Toby at me. "She wants you to go! Mum, have you gone completely mad? She can't even go to the supermarket without crying." Even my insensitive brother could see this was a stupid idea.

I could feel the beast closing in on me. I took some deep breaths, like I did in Fiona's powder blue room, the last time I was there. Deep breaths, like it said in one of the printouts on my bed. I focused on the cool air hitting my nostrils and not on the beast's hold on me. The scent of jasmine drifted in through the open kitchen door. I focused on the air travelling down my throat, filling my lungs and lifting my ribcage. I could feel the oxygen hit my hot brain and ever so very slightly cool and release the tightness in my head. Slowly, I released my breath through my mouth and the beast took a step away from me. It was still there but I was in charge now.

"Sometimes Mum, you just make everything worse for this family!" Toby yelled and stormed off.

"One day when you're a parent you'll understand Toby!" Mum shouted after him. He slammed the front door behind him and still Mum, illogically, kept shouting after him because he couldn't hear, "I am trying to do the right thing for my daughter because I love her!"

I took another deep breath and focused on me and my body. I felt so tense.

Mum rearranged the yellow roses in their vase.

"Drink your lemonade M!" She snapped.

I was still focusing on the tension in my body and I tried to release my tight shoulders and my stiff jaw. Another deep breath and I could feel the beast's cold eyes avert its gaze from me. It lowered its head and walked out of the room. I took another deep, centring breath.

"I don't want to go to this school Mum," I said.

Mum sighed.

"Look, it was just an idea. There's no pressure M. Your dad and I thought it might make you happy. That's all. No one's going to force you to go to a school you don't want to go to." And she went over to the fridge and rearranged her magnets. "It was just a thought really."

She'd listened to me. Mum's actually heard me and the beast...it's gone too. I suspected it wasn't too far away and could be lurking behind the door or hiding outside the window but I couldn't see it or sense it. I felt fine and I didn't want Mum to ask me any more questions or Toby to slam any more doors. I didn't want the phone to ring, a text to beep or anything else to be said. I just wanted to enjoy feeling fine. I took some more deep breaths. Mum stopped fiddling with the "life is a journey" magnet and looked at me, puzzled.

"Are you OK M?" she asked. "You seem a bit...different."

"I'm fine." Even if it was just for a few moments, I felt fine. And I wondered is that what normal felt like?

"I'm going to my room," I said and I sensed her getting worried that I was going to hide under the duvet or cry but I wasn't, so I told her directly, like it said in one of those leaflets. It said,

"Why not try explaining how you are feeling directly and explain what you intend to do, so friends and family understand what's going on in your life?"

So I did try,

"I just want to try on some new combinations of clothes and watch season 3, episode 4 of Skylar again. I'm fine." And as I walk up the stairs Mum went back to her fridge magnets and I heard her saying,

"She's fine. M's fine. My baby's fine."

That night I was in my room. I was playing some tracks from Skylar and singing along. I could hear good noises from downstairs like Mum chatting on her phone, or giggling when she got a text message and she was singing along to some 80s music on the radio. I sat in front of my mirror and said to my reflection,

"Overall it's been a C day." I glanced through the many leaflets and pages on my bed that Mum had been leaving me. At first I wasn't sure about the diagnosis (and I'm still not) but some of the leaflets make sense. Like struggling with getting on public transport and coping with change. There's another leaflet about noise sensitivity, one about autism being a gift (really?) and lots about anxiety,

"Anxiety is a key feature of autism and while it can never be eradicated completely it can be managed. New and different life situations happen to everyone, so it is important for someone living with autism to realise they may need to find new strategies and coping mechanisms throughout life's changes."

Changes. Changes. Changes. The word and all its implications ricocheted round my body and brain, like I'd been shot. I took a deep breath and put the leaflet down.

Strategies...explaining how I really feel, **MOLW**, staying in my bedroom and deep breathing.

Tuesday 4.00pm

"You took control M! I am so proud!" Fiona flings her hands in the air with excitement and whacks her glasses all askew when I tell her about my breathing exercises and the beast leaving the room and me feeling fine for one evening, one night and the following morning.

"I am so proud of you! Oh, you've done so well M!" I actually feel a bit flustered as usually Fiona is always very calm and measured. I've never seen her animated. I think she senses this and she straightens her glasses, settles back into her beige, comfy chair and we have a nice, safe

COUNSELLOR SILENCE

I break the silence.

"Control? I took control?" I question and she nods and repeats it back to me again,

"You took control M."

"But what if I can't take control again on the bus or the English room or when I see Lynx?" I ask, and I feel anxious just thinking about all these things. I take a deep breath.

"The truth is M, you probably won't always be able to take control and anxiety will get the better of you again." And my heart sinks. Fiona sees me deflate.

"But it's best we deal with the truth, then you know how to manage or cope with life's changes and challenges effectively.

And it's so good that we know the breathing exercises can help you."

"The truth…"

"Yes. The truth."

"Like I am an autistic girl."

"Yes. You are a teenage girl who has autism. That is the truth."

COUNSELLOR SILENCE

"I don't like this label, autism," I state.

"Labels make some people think they feel better. Some people feel safe if they label themselves or other people, but you're so much more than a label."

"Yes!" I reply and I'm flapping my hands now because I'm excited. I like this! Fiona is stating the truth. "That's right!" I start to speak really quickly. I'm excited because she really understands me! "Sometimes people don't know what to do with me and I think Mum's really happy that I fit in with this new, autistic girl label but I am so much more than that."

Fiona is nodding.

"It's like I can be shelved correctly or put in the right section. I mean, do people know what being autistic is? The truth is they don't really know me. I wonder if they really knew me they might get scared, so it's easy for them to say, 'She's autistic' and label me but the truth is they have no idea of the shape, texture and size of my world."

COUNSELLOR SILENCE

You are a wonderful teenage girl

said Fiona.

And you have autism. The truth is, you will need some support and guidance with life's inevitable ups and downs but you can have a glorious, fulfilled life M and this is the truth too.

I TOOK A VERY DEEP BREATH.